A CHANCE TO PUT THINGS RIGHT

A SHORT STORY
BY
THOMAS MAYNES

To my parents, Timothy and Brigitte

1

Changing the past could greatly improve the present. So thought Michael Fernsby as he sat at his desk in the Ministry of Defence building in Whitehall, reading a report on the ongoing Soviet civil war. Looking out the window, he saw the River Thames and the London skyline beyond. How serene the city looked. So few of its people had any idea of how much danger they were in.

The year 2005 was looking to be one of the most turbulent in history. After sixty years of Cold War, the Eastern Bloc had finally collapsed in on itself. Violence had broken out not only in the Soviet Union itself but in several of its satellite states. No one was quite sure of the death toll, but it was likely to be catastrophically high. And it was not only the East that was suffering the consequences of these civil wars. The destabilisation had resulted in very dangerous weapons falling into the hands of very dangerous terrorist and insurgent groups. There was now an unsettling rumour going around the Ministry of Defence that the security services had good intelligence that a nuclear attack on London was being planned.

Michael tried not to worry about the rumour, but he could not help but wonder if events might have played out differently under different circumstances. He did not believe there had been anything inevitable about the Eastern European conflicts. It was a shame, he mused, that he did not have a time machine. If such things existed, he was sure he could change the world for the better.

"Michael Fernsby?" These words brought him out of his train of thought. The thirty-one-year-old civil servant tore his gaze away from the window and turned to face the speaker. She was a woman Michael knew by face but to whom he had never spoken.

"Yes, that's me. Can I help you?"

"I wonder if I could have a word with you in my office."

Michael followed the woman, who he was pretty sure was quite senior in the MoD, out of the open plan office and into a lift, which took them to an unfamiliar floor. The woman never introduced herself, but the nameplate on her office door read "Priya Begum". Begum motioned Michael to a seat before taking her own behind the desk. Michael could not help but feel nervous. He had absolutely no idea why he had been summoned here. Fortunately, Begum wasted no time in explaining.

"As I expect you're aware," she began, "earlier this week NATO forces in Czechoslovakia rescued four Western prisoners who were being held by the Czechoslovak government on behalf of the Soviets." Michael was indeed aware. His security clearance was not the highest but things got around the MoD quickly enough, and right now everyone was talking about the British military campaigns in the former Warsaw Pact.

Begum continued. "Two of them are American, one is French and the fourth, it seems, is British. He calls himself Jack Smith, although we don't think that's his real name, and he claims to have been held for twenty-four years. The trouble is that we can't find any record of a missing British man meeting his description. As far as we can tell, he's neither ex-military nor ex-intelligence. He's refusing to give us any useful information regarding his identity or the circumstances of his capture."

"What's this got to do with me?" The words were out of Michael's mouth before he realised. Begum did not seem to be put off by the abruptness.

"Smith, or whatever his name is, is currently undergoing treatment in Barts and we'd like you to speak with him. We think you might be more successful than anyone else in getting him to open up."

"Why would I be any help?" asked Michael.

There was a brief pause. Then Begum leant forward and said something unexpected.

"Because he asked for you personally."

2

A government car took Michael the short distance from Whitehall to the hospital. The brief journey gave him a little time to take in what was happening. Begum had been quite clear; Smith had asked specifically for Michael. He could not even begin to imagine why this man would want to speak with him or even how he knew of his existence. If Smith was telling the truth, then Michael had only been seven years old at the time of his capture.

What worried him most was what his superiors would think. After all, it did not look good that a man who had been held by the Soviets for over two decades knew the name of a particular civil servant in the Ministry of Defence. Michael had never even dreamt of betraying his country, but he was very aware that this whole business cast him in a suspicious light. This, of course, made it even more important that he convince Smith to speak up. He had a personal stake in it.

The car radio, meanwhile, was broadcasting live coverage of Parliament, which had been recalled from its summer recess. The Leader of the Opposition was criticising the Prime Minister's handling of the current crisis. Such arguments, particularly over British military involvement in Eastern Europe, had dominated discourse in the House of Commons over the past few months. Michael would usually be taking careful note of the proceedings, but today he was too busy worrying about his upcoming meeting to pay attention to the usual back-and-forth between the Right Honourable Member for Enfield Southgate and the Right Honourable Member for Brent East.

Before long, the car arrived at St Bartholomew's Hospital in the City of London and Michael entered through King Henry's gate. Smith had a room to himself and Michael could not help but notice the policeman stationed at the door. He had a feeling that Smith would not be allowed to leave even if he so desired.

The patient was dozing when Michael arrived. Smith looked to be in his mid-fifties. His greying hair appeared as though it had not been cut recently and his face was obscured by an untidy beard. Michael closed the door behind him before speaking.

"Excuse me, Mr Smith?" Smith woke with a start and stared intently at Michael for a few seconds before his face broke into a smile.

"Michael Fernsby," he replied, "it's good to see you."

"Have we met before?" Michael sat in a chair next to the bed and surveyed the other man. There was certainly something familiar about him but it was difficult to pinpoint what.

"I suppose not," was Smith's vague reply.

"Then why did you ask to see me?"

"Because you're the only one I can really trust." He stared into space for a few moments before saying, "How are things at the MoD?"

The change of subject took Michael by surprise. "About as well as can be expected," was the only response that came to mind.

"I imagine it's very hectic at the moment."

"You could say that."

"It's all a bit of a mess, isn't it? Civil war in the Soviet Union, shots fired between West and East Germany, NATO forces involved in two Eastern European revolutions, and the whole thing has led to a wave of international terrorism."

"You're well informed for someone who's been a prisoner for so long." As soon as he spoke, Michael became worried that his words might have been insensitive. Smith, however, did not seem offended.

"Oh, I was given a surprising amount of access to news literature, particularly in the latter years. They even sometimes provided me with copies of the Times and the Economist. Can I ask you something, Michael?"

"Of course."

"Do you like the world the way it is?"

Michael paused to think. "That's a very complicated question." The honest answer was no; he did not like the world as it was. "It's certainly become a very dangerous place of late," was his eventual answer. "Why do you ask?"

"Because it should be different. Michael,

there's something you need to know, something I've got to make you understand. This isn't how things are supposed to be. The world is wrong and it's all my fault."

"What are you talking about?"

"History has unfolded differently than it should have from a point of divergence in 1981. I know because I caused that point of divergence. This is not the 2005 I knew."

"Are you trying to tell me that you…?"

"Travelled in time? Yes."

Michael did not know how to respond. His first thought was that the other man was joking, but there was something very serious about Smith's demeanour. He had, of course, been held captive for almost two and a half decades. It was possible that the experience had affected his mind more than the doctors had realised.

"You don't believe me," Smith said with no hint of surprise. "Will you at least hear me out?"

Michael was losing hope that this conversation would be of any use. Then again, he was still hoping that Smith would be able to exonerate him. "Why don't you tell me the whole story?"

"I'm from what can be best described as an alternate timeline, or alternate reality if you prefer. The world in my reality was different to this one in many ways. One of the key differences was that the communist revolution in Pakistan never happened. As a result, the Soviet invasion of Afghanistan went far less smoothly and the USSR never established an effective power base in the Middle East. In my reality, a man called Mikhail Gorbachev became General Secretary of the Soviet Communist Party in 1985. I won't bore you with the details but Gorbachev initiated a series of reforms that ultimately led to the fall of the Communist Party and the dissolution of the Soviet Union in 1991. With this came the overthrow of all other communist governments in Eastern Europe. The Berlin Wall came down in 1989 and the Cold War effectively ended soon after. This all happened relatively peacefully. That's the world in which I grew up. My entire adult life, up until I went back in time, was spent in a post-Cold War era.

"When I was in my early thirties, I was part of a government team tasked with studying a mysterious device that was found by research scientists in the British Antarctic Territory. My role was mainly administrative to be honest, but it was fascinating work. We never discovered the origins of the device but we did discover its function: time travel. I know it sounds insane but this device was capable of sending a person into the past and into the future. We experimented with it for months, always careful to avoid making any changes to the timeline.

"I gather there was much debate amongst our superiors about what to do with the device. It was eventually decided that it was too dangerous to be kept intact. I was ordered to destroy it, and I might have done if it weren't for the London bombings."

"Which ones?" asked Michael.

"None of the ones you're thinking of," Smith

replied. "It was an attack that, in my timeline, would have happened only a few weeks ago. On the seventh of July 2005, a militant Islamist organisation called al-Qaeda launched a series of coordinated suicide bombings in London. Fifty-two people were killed. And it wasn't an isolated event. They had carried out several similar and even bigger attacks since the 1990s, including an attack on New York's World Trade Center in 2001."

"I've never heard of them."

"Well of course you haven't but, in my reality, they were responsible for countless deaths. And, with the device, I was presented with a unique opportunity to do something about it."

"By… going back in time?" Michael was finding this story more and more tedious by the minute.

"Exactly. Al-Qaeda was led by a Saudi Arabian named Osama bin Laden, who started his paramilitary career as an insurgent against the Soviets in Afghanistan. In the early '80s he lived in Peshawar, a city in northern Pakistan, near the Afghan border. I used the device to travel back to August 1981. I then journeyed to Peshawar, where I assassinated bin Laden. The idea was to prevent al-Qaeda from ever being founded and, in that respect, I was successful.

"But something happened for which I couldn't have prepared. I planted a timed bomb, which I'd acquired illegally in the present, in the house where bin Laden was staying. Little did I know that in that house was a stolen nuclear device, which was set off by my bomb. The resulting explosion was devastating."

"*You* caused the Peshawar Blast?" exclaimed Michael, momentarily forgetting that he did not believe Smith's tale. "If that's true then you're a mass murderer."

"I *am* a mass murderer, but not just because of Peshawar. My actions that day indirectly killed millions.

"Fortunately for me, I wasn't in range of the nuclear blast. I attempted to make my escape through Afghanistan but I was picked up by Afghan communists and handed over to the Soviets. They were under the impression that I was a British agent. I spent the next twenty-four years being passed around various detention facilities. Once they realised that I didn't have any useful information to tell them, they stopped trying.

"It didn't take me long to realise that I'd changed history far more than I'd intended, but by then it was too late. The Peshawar Blast destabilised the Pakistani government enough to facilitate a successful communist revolution. This greatly strengthened the USSR's position in the Middle East and led to the defeat of anti-Soviet insurgents in the region. In this new timeline, Gorbachev never came to power and his reforms never took place. This significantly delayed the fall of communism in the Eastern Bloc.

"You know the rest, of course. The Cold War continued into the twenty-first century and the Soviet Union eventually collapsed into civil war, followed by its satellite states. I caused the world to be far worse than it was before. I had come to accept that I'd never be able to fix it, but then I was rescued. And now I owe it to the world to sort out the mess I've made."

Michael was not sure what to make of Smith's story. It was certainly detailed. Smith did not seem to be out of his mind, and yet there could not possibly be any truth in what he was saying. He could simply be lying, of course, but what would be his motive for that?

"So, tell me, who was the Prime Minister in this alternate reality of yours?" was all he could think of to say.

"Tony Blair," was Smith's reply.

"Tony Blair? As in the Defence Secretary?"

"Does that surprise you?"

"A little. It's not that he isn't a competent minister. I just can't imagine him becoming leader of the Conservative Party."

"Labour."

"I'm sorry?"

"In my timeline, Blair led a *Labour* government."

"How on earth did that happen?"

"Every changed event has a knock-on effect, Michael. The different international situation inevitably impacted domestic politics. In my timeline, Margaret Thatcher won a third term in 1987. Neil Kinnock was never Prime Minister and the Conservatives took longer to embrace social libertarianism.

The hard left didn't take over the Labour Party and the mass defection of centrists to the Tories in the '90s never happened. In my reality, Blair brought Labour to the centre ground and by now was starting his third term in office."

"I see…" Michael's morning had ended up being much more interesting than he had expected. Smith was very unusual but that was understandable. What Michael still could not work out was why *he* specifically had been summoned. Smith had said that Michael was the only person he could trust. Why could that be? He decided to ask as much. "What am I doing here, Mr Smith?"

"That's not my real name."

"You don't say."

"You're here because I knew you were the person who I stood the best chance of convincing to help me."

"Why?"

"Oh Michael, haven't you worked it out yet? Look at me."

"What are you talking…"

"Look me in the eyes, Michael!"

Michael did look. Smith's blue, unblinking eyes looked back at him; the same eyes he saw every day in the mirror. The realisation must have shown on his face because Smith smiled. "Do you believe me now?" he asked.

The room seemed to be spinning as Michael moved his gaze to each of the other man's facial features in turn. He felt like he was dreaming. Soon he could take it no more and, without saying another word, he jumped to his feet and ran out of the room.

3

Michael sat on a bench facing the fountain in the St Bartholomew's main square. The more he tried to get his head around the situation, the more confused he became. He could not believe how long it had taken him to notice that Smith looked just like him. Older, of course, and the beard hid some of his features, but other than that he was a doppelgänger. Not only that but he sounded the same. Michael had heard enough recordings of his own voice over the years to know what it sounded like, and Smith's voice matched it exactly.

But how could the story be true? Michael had often thought about the concept of time travel but he had never in his entire life entertained the notion that it was actually possible, nor that he would ever witness its effects first hand. He wondered whether he was going insane. Perhaps the whole conversation had been a hallucination, a symptom of a complete mental breakdown. Another possibility was that the whole thing was an elaborate trick, either a light-hearted hoax or something more sinister. But neither of those explanations quite rang true. It had been far too realistic to be a prank and, as Michael calmed down, he became relatively sure that he had not hallucinated. He sat and thought for a long time and, eventually, his head cleared enough that he was able to decide what to do.

He returned to the private room. The man who was not called Smith looked up as he entered. Michael once again closed the door so that they could speak in private, but he remained standing as he addressed the other man.

"What was the name of my first teacher in primary school?"

"Mrs Wilson," came the confident reply. He was right.

Michael tried another question. "Where did I go on my first ever foreign holiday?"

"The south of France, when you were five." That was right as well. Michael thought for a moment. Those questions were too easy. They were things that someone could find out if they tried hard enough. He needed to ask about something really personal; something no one but him could possibly know.

"When I was seven, a couple of months before your supposed point of divergence, my school got a new headmaster. I didn't like him much. He scared me. In fact, he reminded me of someone..."

The other man chuckled before responding. "He reminded you of the Master from Doctor Who," he said. "You... *we* never told that to anyone else."

Michael sat back down in the chair next to the bed, finally convinced. After a brief pause, the older Michael spoke again. "I understand your scepticism. I don't think I'd ever have believed that time travel was possible if I hadn't done it myself."

"I'm still confused."

"I imagine so. What else would you like to know?"

The younger Michael thought for a few seconds as he attempted to organise his thoughts. "So," he began, "you travelled back in time and changed history. In doing so, you prevented the version of you from the new timeline, me, from going back in time."

"Yes," replied older-Michael. "Not only was the reason for my meddling eliminated but you, in this timeline, weren't even given the opportunity."

"Right," continued younger-Michael, "so if that's the case, why are you still here?"

"What do you mean?"

"If your time travelling stopped me from time travelling then the change shouldn't have happened. It's a paradox."

Older-Michael let out a sigh before answering. "You've been watching too much sci-fi. If there's one thing about time travel that you definitely have to understand it's that there's no such thing as a time paradox."

"There isn't?"

"Of course there isn't. It doesn't work like that and there's no reason to think that it should. Various works of fiction have drummed into people the idea that time travel inevitably causes paradoxes but that's completely nonsensical, as you just pointed out. Paradoxes are impossible. The fact that paradoxes are possible under your logic is surely evidence that that logic is flawed."

"OK, fair enough. But then how *does* it work?"

"Simple. When I travelled back in time, I became part of the new timeline but my origins are in the old one. Changing history didn't cause me to disappear any more than demolishing a factory would cause the goods produced in that factory to disappear."

"So what happened to the other timeline?"

"It's gone; replaced with this one. It's the same universe. I just changed it."

"So if you change things back then this timeline will be gone?"

"Correct."

"I don't think I like the idea of that." Younger-Michael had seen the potential benefits of time travel when it was only theoretical but, now it was a reality, he was less sure that he wanted his life erased and replaced.

"Well, I suppose that's understandable." Older-Michael seemed to be considering his words carefully. "You have to remember that this is an alternate reality. The world isn't the way it's supposed to be."

"Maybe to you it isn't, but it is to me. You call this an alternate reality but that's a matter of perspective. As far as the people of this timeline are concerned, this is real. What makes you think you have the right to change it?"

"I didn't say it isn't real. This is absolutely

real. And I understand your reluctance to undo the world you know, but I need you to trust that I know what I'm doing."

"You presumably thought you knew what you were doing before."

"That's a fair point. I made a mistake, a big one, but now I've seen both possibilities, which means I'm in the best position to know what to do. I was naïve and arrogant to think that I could change things without there being any negative consequences. I realise now that the effects of time travel are near impossible to predict and so I shouldn't have messed around with it. All I know for certain is that this timeline is worse than the old one. I can't solve all the world's problems but I can return it to a better state of affairs... if you'll help me."

"How do you know your timeline was the original?" asked younger-Michael. "If time travel is possible, how do you know history hasn't been changed countless times before?"

"I suppose I don't," older-Michael replied with a slight chuckle. "But, since that's completely beyond my control, there's no point worrying about it. I also can't guarantee that everything will be better when I change things back. In fact, it's almost certain that some things will be worse. But it's my judgement that the world will be a better place on the whole. Think of it like that. For every good thing you stand to lose, there's a bad thing that might be improved."

Younger-Michael pondered that whilst the

two sat in silence for a few minutes. Although he had often despaired at the state of the world, he had rarely given much thought to the state of his own life. He did not consider himself to be particularly badly off. He was unmarried and lived alone, but that did not bother him. He had a reasonable job. Cynical as he was about global affairs, personally speaking he was relatively untouched by trauma.

The main exception, his biggest exposure to death in his personal life, had been the tragic loss of the McAllen family when he was twelve years old. Mr and Mrs McAllen were old friends of Michael's parents. They had owned a large farm in Surrey, which Michael had fond memories of visiting during the school holidays. Their daughter, Catherine, was Michael's age. All three of them had died when a passenger plane they were on was shot down, supposedly in error, by militant rebels in Poland. A major international incident had ensued. He wondered what became of Catherine and her parents in the other timeline.

"Did the McAllens die in your reality?"

"The plane crash that killed them never happened, if that's what you're asking." Younger-Michael's surprise at older-Michael's knowledge of the incident must have shown on his face. "As I said, I was given a fair amount of news literature. I saw their names on the list of the dead. But you shouldn't focus too much on individual things. What I'm trying to do is make a general improvement to the world. And to do that I have to travel back in time again and stop myself from messing things up."

"But you're choosing who lives and who dies. You want to save some lives at the expense of others. I don't think I could make that call."

"I know. This is the thought that's haunted me for twenty-four years. I know for a fact that there are people in New York who are alive now but would have died in the old timeline; and that's just one example. I *am* playing God; I know that. My reality was rife with terrorism, wars, even genocides. This isn't a responsibility I would want anyone else to bear, which is why I intend to bear it myself. I made my bed; now I must lie in it.

"OK," said younger-Michael, "if, and I stress *if*, I agree to help you, it's all academic anyway. I have no idea where this device is. Unlike you, I was never recruited into a research team."

"It's quite possible that the device of this timeline was never discovered at all," older-Michael replied, "but that doesn't matter. I'm going to use the device I brought with me from my reality."

"The Soviets didn't take it off you?"

"I didn't take it to Pakistan with me. I hid it before I left Britain. I wasn't sure if I'd survive my plan, and I definitely didn't want an object like that to fall into the wrong hands. I figured it was better to leave it somewhere safe. It's funny that you should mention the McAllens because it was on their estate in Surrey that I buried it. It was a place I knew well enough that I could be sure of finding the device again. I managed to get it in the ground without anyone spotting me. I don't know who owns the land now but I reckon there's a pretty good chance that the device is still there. All I need you to do is retrieve it and bring it to me. I'll handle the rest."

"Why do you need me at all?"

"Oh, come on! Do you really think I could just walk out of here? I've noticed the guard on the door and I'm pretty sure the British government isn't finished with me. Once I have the device that won't be a problem, but until then I'm dependent on you. I can give you directions to the exact place you need to dig."

"I'm still not sure about..."

"Don't think I'm above begging. I know you have misgivings. They're completely understandable. But this is *so* important. I thought I'd messed the world up for good but now I finally have a chance to put things right. Please help me, Michael."

His desperation was obvious. After a long pause, older-Michael looked his younger self in the eyes and a slight smile appeared on his face. "Come on, Michael, who can you trust if not yourself?"

4

The device was not what Michael had expected; not that he had had any idea what to expect. Rectangular in shape and bronze in colour, it measured approximately four inches by two. It had the remains of a broken strap that looked as though it were meant to attach to the wrist or arm. The device's controls, a series of dials, were fixed in place and seemed to require a screwdriver to adjust. Its most striking feature, however, was a deep red, glass hemisphere, which, for some reason, Michael could not quite bring himself to look at closely.

The device had been buried exactly where the older Michael had said it would be. After leaving the hospital, the younger Michael had returned to work and put off Begum by telling her that he had learned nothing useful. Then, that very evening, he had driven to the Surrey countryside. At the dead of night, he entered the farm once owned by the McAllens and found the exact spot to which his older self had directed him. At the top of a slope, on the edge of a field stood an old oak tree. Michael dug at the foot of this tree and found a metal box, inside of which was the strange instrument that could apparently be used to travel in time. He was back at his ground-floor flat in Walthamstow before daybreak.

Michael now had in his possession a truly remarkable object. He could not help but wonder where and when it had been made, and by whom. It was unlikely that he would ever know. Regardless, the amount of power at his disposal was immense. Part of him felt he should turn the device over to the authorities. Another part felt that he should destroy it. And then, of course, there was the option of giving it back to his older self as requested. He had avoided committing himself, telling older-Michael that he would have to think it over. After calling in sick to work, he set about doing just that.

It was clear that older-Michael passionately believed that restoring the previous timeline was the right thing to do. Younger-Michael did not doubt his sincerity, nor the goodness of his intentions. But he was still very reluctant to change what was to him the genuine reality. True though it was that the world was undergoing an incredibly destructive upheaval, he was not convinced that he had the right to erase and replace the lives of so many people. Not only that but, if his older self's tale demonstrated anything, it was that time travel could have unforeseen consequences. What if older-Michael's attempt to change things back just made the world worse still?

For the second time in as many days, he thought about his old friend. Older-Michael had said the plane crash that had killed Catherine never happened in his timeline. It had been nineteen years since she died, but Michael could still clearly remember her smile and her laugh. They had only been children, but she had meant a lot to him; more than he had ever been brave enough to tell her. She was the kindest and most thoughtful person he had ever known. She had not deserved to die so young.

But his older self had also cautioned him against thinking about time travel that way. He had said he wanted to improve the whole world, not help individual people. But how could Michael possibly judge such things? As he sat in his flat in the mid-morning, he was still at a loss as to what to do.

Then, all of a sudden, something happened that changed everything. Just after half past ten, a tactical nuclear weapon, planted near the National Theatre, was detonated. The damage was unbelievable. The radius of destruction was about one and a half miles, the result of which was that over seven square miles of central London, including Westminster and the City, was destroyed. Gone were the seat of the British government, the Houses of Parliament, countless residential estates and, of course, St Bartholomew's Hospital, where Michael's older self had been.

Michael stayed in his flat as the authorities and emergency services attempted futilely to deal with the situation. The news reported that the weapon used was believed to have fallen into terrorists' hands from the Soviet arsenal. The death toll was already estimated in the hundreds of thousands. Those members of the government who had survived were on the television insisting that the situation could be controlled, that the United Kingdom would live on, but it was clear that the country was crumbling.

Michael was in tears as all of this unfolded. The collapse of Eastern Europe had finally impacted Britain in a catastrophic way. That it had all been indirectly caused by an alternate version of him only added to his devastation. He could no longer deny the magnitude of what was happening. The world was falling apart and there was nothing anyone could do to stop it; anyone except for him.

He picked up the device and held it in front of him. The settings had presumably not been changed since the other version of him had used it last and so, he reasoned, it was already set to take him to 1981. He had never been given instructions regarding the activation of the device but he had a feeling that he did not need them.

Fighting his aversion, he looked into the glass hemisphere. As he did so, it began to glow bright red. He looked deeper and started to see patterns and shapes. They were mesmerising. Soon it seemed like there was nothing but the patterns. Deeper and deeper he stared until they were all he could perceive. An indeterminate amount of time passed as Michael fell further and further into the trance. When he was totally consumed, he slipped into unconsciousness.

5

Thunderstorms swept across southern England in early August 1981. This was bad news for Michael, who was sleeping rough in a wood in Surrey. The wood in question was on the edge of the field where, twenty-four years in the future, Michael had dug up the time-travel device. That, of course, was the reason he was there.

He had woken up on a construction site, on which his flat was being built. It did not take him long to realise that he had arrived a couple of weeks early. The device was clearly not that accurate, but this actually suited him. He needed to intercept the other Michael before he made any major changes to the timeline. The way to do that was obvious. Michael knew that his alternate self would at some point turn up at the McAllens' estate to bury the device. When that happened, he needed to be ready to intervene. After stealing some supplies, including enough food to survive for a few weeks, he travelled to the Surrey countryside, to the exact spot where he needed to be. There he waited. He had to sleep, of course, and he was terrified that he would miss his opportunity. The fate of the world rested on his shoulders.

One morning in August saw Michael sitting

at the edge of the wood, wrapped in a blanket and watching the old oak tree at the edge of the field. Next to him was a shopping trolley, which he had also stolen and in which were all of his supplies. He was exhausted, he had not washed in a long time and he did not want to think about what he must looked like. The ground was wet from the storm the night before and the sun was rising over the fields and trees as a figure became visible in the distance, walking towards the oak tree. Michael kept low to the ground; he had to stay hidden from employees of the McAllens. As the figure drew closer, however, he saw that it was the alternate version of himself. He had shown up at last.

Michael threw off the blanket and walked briskly out into the open, stopping next to the oak tree. It was not long before the other Michael spotted him. If he was surprised, he did not show it. He simply continued to walk, keeping eye contact as he did so. Michael could not help but notice how gaunt and solemn his alternate self looked, almost as though he were a hollow shell. He had a heavy looking duffle bag over his shoulder, a rucksack on his back and a shovel in his hand.

When he was a few feet away, he stopped. Still without breaking eye contact, he took the duffle bag off his shoulder and gently placed it on the ground. Michael wondered if it contained the bomb with which he intended to blow up his target.

"I suppose I shouldn't be too surprised," the alternate Michael said, and his voice was as solemn as his face. "I *am* messing around with time travel, after all. The question is, are you here to help me or to stop me?"

"To stop you." Michael considered that there was little to be gained from lying.

"That's a pity." The double was still not showing any signs of shock, but the frown had not left his face. This threw Michael but he pushed on with his rehearsed speech.

"Look, I know you think you're doing a good thing, but I can tell you for a fact that you're making a big mistake. I've seen the world you create and it's not an improvement; quite the opposite. I know how determined you are to carry out your plan, but I'm sure you'll understand that I'm better informed than you are and am in a better position to make a judgement."

"If you're a future version of me then you know my motivation."

"I'm not exactly a future version of you. It's complicated. I'm you from the alternate timeline you're about to create. As sure as you are now that you want to change history, I know for certain that you'll live to regret it. I know because you told me yourself many years from now."

"If you have information that can help me then we can work together. If you don't want to do that then get the hell out of my way."

It did not surprise Michael that his double was not easily convinced; after all, he himself had at first been unconvinced by the older version's argument. It had taken a nuclear explosion to change his mind. He decided that now was the time for full disclosure.

"The bomb you plant in Peshawar triggers a nuclear explosion that greatly changes events in the Middle East." As Michael spoke, the double took off his rucksack and began to sort through it as though he were looking for something. Michael started speaking more urgently. "The result is that the Cold War is significantly prolonged and leads to a series of devastating civil wars in Eastern Europe." The double withdrew several objects from the rucksack, including the metal box containing the time-travel device, but continued to search. "The world is destabilised beyond belief and eventually, in 2005, a large part of London is destroyed by a nuclear bomb planted by terrorists." Michael was not sure whether his alternate self was listening anymore. The double finally found what he was looking for in his rucksack.

Michael gasped as he found himself facing a handgun. The shock of being held at gunpoint by a version of himself was something for which he was not prepared. The double had a borderline deranged look on his face and Michael suddenly came to the realisation that there was more to the whole thing than he had thought. His alternate self was not just determined to change history; he was obsessively fixated. The older version in the hospital had explained his motives, but had he told the whole story?

"Don't you dare try to stop me!" the double

snapped. "I've been granted a miracle, a chance to put things right. Whatever the consequences, I won't throw this opportunity away."

The two glared at each other for several seconds before the double lowered the gun and tucked it into the waistband of his trousers. Michael sighed in relief but his reaction was premature. Before he knew what was happening, the other man had swung the shovel with great force and struck the side of his head. He crashed to the ground, blood pouring from his temple, the scenery spinning.

The double strode past and began to dig by the foot of the tree. Michael lay in a daze for a while before regaining his bearings slightly. He crawled on his hands and knees until he came upon the pile of belongings that the double had taken out of his rucksack whilst looking for the gun. Much of it was made up of clothes. There was also a penknife, a wallet and some keys. The thing that drew Michael's attention, however, was a photograph. He took the photograph in his hands and, trying his best to ignore the pain in his head, looked closely at the figures depicted. There were two people, arm in arm. One of them was Michael, or rather the alternate Michael. The other person was a woman Michael did not immediately recognise but who looked strangely familiar, just as the older Michael in the hospital had done. Both figures in the photograph were wearing wedding rings.

"Who's this?" Michael, now kneeling, held the photograph up to his other self, who gave it a momentary glance.

"Fuck off," was the double's blunt response. He continued digging.

"I'm serious. Who is she?" Michael could tell that he had touched a nerve and wondered whether this mysterious woman was the missing piece of the puzzle, part of the reason his other self was so obsessed with changing the timeline.

"Don't try to play mind games with me," the double replied coldly. "If you think you can use Cathy to manipulate me then you're wrong. I'm doing this for her."

"Cathy?" Michael glanced at the ring on his double's finger and then looked again at the photograph. The identity of the woman, nineteen years older than the last time he had seen her, hit him like a ton of bricks. "This is Catherine McAllen! You're married to Catherine McAllen?" The double kept digging and Michael finally understood. "You *were* married to her. She died in the London bombings, at the hands of al-Qaeda. That's why you're doing this. I'm right, aren't I?"

The double nodded. Michael rose to his feet and approached his alternate self. "There's something you need to know," he said in what he hoped was a sensitive tone. "In the timeline you're about to create, Catherine dies in a plane crash at age twelve. The two of us were never together. I know you have your wife's best interests at heart but what you're about to do won't save her." The double stopped digging and looked Michael in the eyes, as though attempting to read his thoughts.

"If you're lying…"

"I swear I'm not. I wasn't messing around when I asked who she was. I genuinely didn't recognise her. I'm so sorry for your loss… but I lost her a long time ago."

The double let his shovel drop to the floor as his frown disappeared, to be replaced by an expression that was somehow even sadder.

"I told myself that I was doing this for the sake of everyone, for the good of the world… but it was mainly for her. I made my decision on the day of her funeral. As I watched them put her coffin in the grave I knew I had to do whatever it took to save her. But maybe her fate was always to die, always to leave me behind." A single tear escaped his eye as he looked straight ahead, beyond the scenery.

"I don't think I believe in fate," Michael replied. "I don't think anything's written in stone. Life's simply impossible to predict, even with the benefit of time travel."

The double turned to look at him. "Maybe I can still fix it. I know what goes wrong now. I can do things differently. If I need to, I can go back in time again and again until I get it right."

"No. That's a bad idea. If there's one thing I've learned, it's that meddling with time causes more problems than it solves. We've been given an almost godlike power but it's ultimately a curse. Every change will have unexpected consequences. We can never be sure of the damage we're causing. The world will never be perfect but it has the potential to be much worse than it is. It's natural to look at all the death and destruction and misery, and long to eradicate it but you never will. It's hard to accept, but time is better left alone. There'll always be pain but there'll also always be happiness. All we can do is hope the latter outweighs the former."

The double gave a slight nod as more tears appeared in his eyes. He put a hand on Michael's shoulder and a smile appeared on his face for the first time.

"Thank you for coming to clean up my mess," he said. "You're a better me than I am. I'm sorry you have to deal with all this. I know the timeline will be safe in your hands."

Michael was momentarily puzzled, but then the meaning of the words became clear as the double, quick as a flash, pulled out the gun and put it to his own head.

"No!" Michael shouted, but it was too late. There was a deafening bang and the double fell to the floor, his body lifeless, his pain finally over.

Michael looked down at the corpse, then at the photograph that was still in his hand. The smiling man in the image had suffered a terrible loss and, naturally, done everything he could to reverse the tragedy. It just happened that he had had a powerful and dangerous resource at his disposal. Michael wished he had been able to save him. He hoped he had at least saved many others.

He knew that his mission was not yet over.

He now possessed two time-travel devices, and he needed to find a way to destroy them. Fortunately, time was on his side. Beyond that, he intended to stay out of history's way. And then, in twenty-four years' time, there was someone he needed to see.

6

Changing the past could greatly improve the present. So thought Michael Fernsby as he watched his wife's coffin being lowered into the ground. Two weeks previously, on the seventh of July 2005, she and dozens of others had been killed in a series of terrorist attacks in London. The world was becoming an ever-darker place. The terrorist organisation to which the instigators of this attack were linked, named al-Qaeda, was responsible for a wave of terror across the world. Most friends and relatives of the victims could do nothing but mourn the tragic loss of their loved ones. Michael, however, had another option.

Unknown to virtually everyone else, he was involved in a top-secret government project centred around a mysterious device discovered in Antarctica. Through much experimentation it had been determined that the device was capable of transporting a person through time. Its destruction had been ordered but Michael had defied that order and smuggled it away. It now rested in the inside pocket of his jacket. Over the past few days, he had grappled with the dilemma before him but, as he stood at the graveside, he had all but made up his mind. Changing history for the better was not only within his power but also his moral duty.

After the conclusion of the service, Michael spoke briefly with the priest as the other people gathered at the graveside began to make their way to the funeral reception. As he conversed, Michael spotted a man standing on his own, looking his way. The man was dressed appropriately for a funeral and Michael thought that he had seen him at the main service in the church. After bidding goodbye to the priest and assuring his straggling relatives that he would follow them shortly, he walked towards the man and greeted him.

"Thank you for coming," Michael said. He concluded that he must have met the man before because he looked familiar. Most likely in his fifties, he had greying hair and was Michael's height. Michael could not, however, remember exactly who he was. "I'm terribly sorry but I'm having trouble placing you. What's your name?"

"You can call me Jack Smith," the man replied. "I'm very sorry for your loss."

"Thank you, Jack. Did you know Catherine well?"

"I did a long time ago but I've been overseas for several years. I wanted to pay my respects, but I'm also here to see how you are, Michael. How are you managing? Are you OK?"

Michael was about to respond with his well-practiced line, that he was coping, but there was something about Smith that made him reluctant to lie. He felt he did not need to answer the question at all. The other man already seemed to know that Michael was *not* coping.

Jack Smith spoke again. "Why don't you sit for a few minutes? I'm a pretty good listener." The two of them sat down on a nearby bench and looked ahead over the graveyard.

It was difficult to pinpoint but Smith had a comforting quality that appealed to Michael. Although he was not a friend, nor even an acquaintance, there was something reassuring about him. His concerned yet detached demeanour stood in stark contrast to that of everyone else in Michael's life. So far, none of the people who had attempted to console him had succeeded in diminishing his ever-increasing anger.

"I feel like I've been robbed of my future," he began. "A part of me is dead. No matter how hard I try, I can't imagine a life without her."

There was a short pause before Smith replied. "The world is certainly cruel. It's difficult for me to put myself in your exact position, but I imagine you're feeling very let down by the universe." Michael nodded. "Someone in your position would be justified in wanting to alter events, fix the world... change the past."

"What?" Michael turned to face the other man as the implications of his words sunk in. Smith's presence, and this conversation, suddenly seemed more orchestrated. This was not a chance encounter. He knew what was going on. Perhaps Michael's superiors were on to him after all. His concerns evidently showed on his face because Smith was quick to assuage his fears.

"I'm not from the government," he said quickly. "I'm a bit like you; mixed up in time travel. As honourable as your intentions are, you're about to make a big mistake. I had to come and warn you. I know how bizarre this sounds, but it's the truth."

"I believe you," said Michael. It was true. Now he knew that time travel was possible, he was completely receptive to the idea of intervention from the future. That was, after all, what he was planning himself. With that in mind, Smith's familiarity with Michael's situation made a bit more sense.

"I'm not here to judge you," Smith continued. "I'm not here to fight you. I'm here to help you. I know you have access to the time-travel device and that you're considering using it. I've come to ask you to let me destroy it. My involvement in all this is complicated but I very much have the benefit of hindsight. I know how determined you are, but I understand all this far better than you do. I'm asking you to trust that I know what's best." Smith waited for his words to sink in. After a while he spoke again. "I can deal with the device. All I need you to do is direct me to where you've hidden it."

"That won't be necessary," Michael replied. Slowly, he reached into his jacket and withdrew the bronze-coloured device with its distinctive red hemisphere. He still knew so little about it. Its origins and history were a complete mystery. Nevertheless, it gave him an unbelievable power, one that he was reluctant to relinquish. For several seconds he held the device in his hand, unsure of what to do.

Smith broke the silence. "I know how you feel. As someone who's lost a lot of loved ones, I can see the appeal of altering time. I need you to trust me when I tell you that changing the past will not make things better, and it won't save Cathy's life. Rolling the dice with history isn't worth it. I know you don't want to have to live with what's happened but I promise you it will get easier with time." Smith held out his hand. "Give it to me, Michael... please."

Michael looked down at the device, running his thumb over its glass hemisphere and many dials. "This is my one chance," he said, more to himself than to Smith. "Will any other human being ever have this opportunity to make the world a better place?" Michael looked up, meeting Smith's gaze, and the older man's face conveyed more understanding and empathy than anyone else had been able to show him.

"Believe me when I say I know you very well. You think your life isn't worth living if you can't save her. I'm here to tell you that you're wrong. You don't have to mess with time to make the world a better place. Your duty is to strive to improve *this* reality, not to create a new, potentially worse one. To do that, you need to let go of the past."

After the briefest of pauses that nevertheless felt like a lifetime, Michael placed the device in Smith's outstretched hand.

"Thank you, Michael. I think you know this is

the right thing to do." Without waiting another second, Smith withdrew a small screwdriver from his pocket and examined the device.

"We think there's a self-destruct mechanism," said Michael.

"I know," replied Smith. "I've done this before. Like I said, I got mixed up in time travel. I ended up with two of these devices in my possession, and I spent years figuring out how to destroy them." Using the screwdriver, he adjusted each dial on the device, carefully making sure that they were all in the place he wanted them. As soon as the last dial was in place, the hemisphere lit up and the whole thing started to vibrate.

Smith got to his feet and walked to the path that wound through the graveyard. Michael followed him. Smith placed the device on the ground and the two men watched as it began to glow incandescently. The glow got brighter and brighter until the device was completely obscured. Less than a minute later there was nothing left but a burn mark on the ground.

"What just happened?" Michael asked.

"I'm still not entirely sure," Smith replied, "but it's definitely gone."

"I can see that." Michael stared at the burn mark, all that was left of the only chance he had had to save Catherine. To his surprise, he did not regret his decision but the finality of it was still unsettling.

Smith could clearly tell what was going through his mind. "You made the right choice. Even if you had somehow managed to save Cathy, the version of her you saved would not have been the Cathy you'd known. Every experience influences the person one becomes. She'd have been an alternate version, a double. The only place your wife can truly live on is in your memory. That's where she'll always be."

Those words brought a slight smile to Michael's face; his first smile in two weeks. "Thank you," were the only words that came out of his mouth as he looked into Smith's familiar blue eyes and suddenly felt a lot less angry with the world.

"Goodbye Michael. You're going to be all right." With those words, Smith turned around and walked away. Michael briefly considered going after him and demanding to know who he was, but he thought better of it. Some things were better left a mystery and perhaps the identity of his guardian angel was one of them. Besides, he had a funeral reception to attend.

Michael turned on his heel and walked towards the church hall, in which his friends and family were waiting. As he did so, his thoughts returned to his wife.

The End